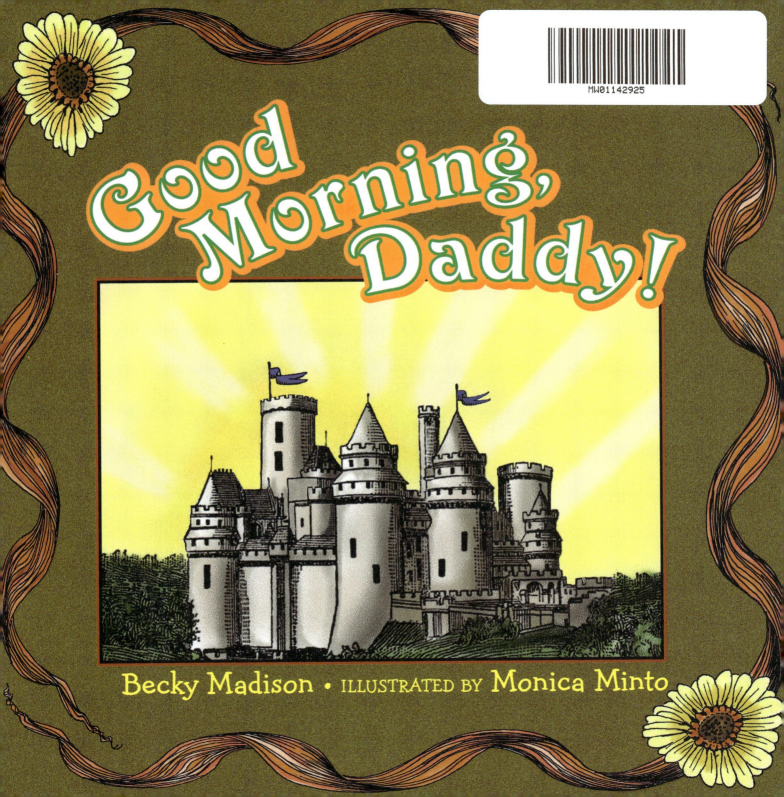

Good Morning, Daddy!

Becky Madison • ILLUSTRATED BY Monica Minto

"My Ribera",
I love you my
second daughter!
Becky Madison

Dedication!

To Jessie Susie:
Thank you for making me a blessed Momma,
and for bringing life to Pillow Bear and Cody.

One magnificently sunny morning, the little princess woke to the ever-so-pleasant sounds she was accustomed to hearing every morning in the castle. It was going to be a busy day as she remembered her father would be entertaining a host of guests later on. Instead of leaping out of bed as she normally would have, she decided to snuggle into the downy folds of the hand-stitched quilt that draped across her four-poster bed.

"What shall I do today?" she contemplated, with her chubby little fingers stroking the pink satin sheets next to her neck and face.

"I think I would like to spend the whole day doing all my favorite things! I want to play with my dollies, read the new storybook I got for my birthday, and go for a long walk with Mommy in the garden! But first, I want to see Daddy and wish him a good morning! He loves me very much!"

Immediately the princess slipped feet first from the high bed until she landed in the ornate, plush carpet covering the polished wooden floors. She wriggled her toes and giggled, as if she had never felt its softness before.

The little princess thought about the many royal subjects who would be visiting her father that day.

"If I am going to see Daddy today, I must prepare myself, just like everyone else. They will be wearing their very best and will stand before him, waiting to be recognized. I better get dressed and ready before I go. No one would dare go before the king in anything but his or her very finest!" she thought. For some reason she was feeling very grown up that morning and decided to act like a big-girl princess.

"I will dress myself and go see my daddy in the throne room," she thought, as she planned her morning.

As she crossed the room toward the antique wardrobe that held all her favorite dresses, she spied her abandoned tea set on the child-sized table. The table was covered with a white, pristinely pressed linen cloth, and was laid with teacups, saucers, creamer, a sugar bowl, a teapot, and silver teaspoons. The dishes were a miniature version of the royal china found on the king's dining table every day, and the teaspoons carried the family crest. In two of the three chairs sat her favorite friends: her very first teddy bear (threadbare in the tummy from lots of hugs) and a brown, long-eared, stuffed puppy that often got in trouble because he was a bit of a rebel. The third chair was empty because the afternoon before, she'd left the tea party earlier than expected.

"Oh, I am so sorry I left you both waiting so long! Shall we finish our tea now? I hope it hasn't gotten too cold. Allow me to pour each of you some more." She offered tea to her most trusted companions.

Without hesitation the little princess sat down in the third chair and began to serve her guests. They engaged themselves in a delightful conversation, discussing many topics, including how they had slept, the weather, how much they enjoyed the new cookies the baker had prepared for them, and why they did not take the time to share tea together more often.

After quite a bit more time had passed than she realized, the little princess threw her hands to her face and cried, "Oh, my goodness, I really must go! I want to wish Daddy good morning before all his guests arrive, and I haven't even dressed yet! Please forgive me! When I return we will continue our chat, and we can decide on a date for our next get-together."

She wiped her lips with the delicate napkin and pushed her chair back under the table before she scurried to the wardrobe to choose her gown for the day.

As most young princesses would, this little royal had an impressive collection of dresses for every occasion. She often delighted in changing her outfits multiple times per day, as her mood or the activity dictated.

"I want to wear my prettiest gown to greet Daddy this morning," she reminded herself. "Which one should I choose to make him happy?"

Spying an old favorite on the bottom of the wardrobe, the little princess pulled out a lovely yellow dress with a white pinafore.

"I haven't seen this one in a very long time," she announced as she slid both pieces on and struggled to tie the large bow behind her back. As she straightened out the wrinkles, she spotted a very large stain on the skirt front.

"Oh, my goodness! I forgot I spilled juice on this, and the spot never came out completely. This will never do!"

She stood on her tiptoes and reached up to slide her favorite pale pink brocade dress with puffy sleeves off the hanger.

"This one is easy to put on," she said. But as she pulled it over her head, she heard a rip that could only mean trouble.

"Oh, no! I will have to fix this. Mommy has been teaching me how to sew, and Daddy will be so very pleased if I show him that I can do it all by myself!" She hummed a little tune as she attempted to mend the seam that held the skirt to the bodice.

"Dear me," she sighed. "I don't think I am doing a very tidy job of this." After quite a while of stitching and then ripping out her work, the little princess gave up and decided to make a third choice.

"I will just have to borrow one of my big sister's gowns," she declared. "Daddy will have to understand."

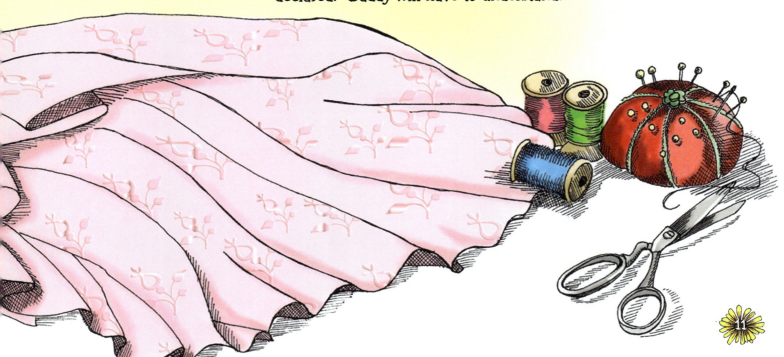

Within just a few moments, the young princess found a grown-up gown in her sister's wardrobe. The dress was many inches too long, and the floral print was much too large for a little girl. She was only able to get the zipper closed just above her waist but was becoming weary from all the failed attempts.

"Since I am wearing Sissy's dress, I think I shall just borrow a pair of her shoes," she decided. She deliberated over which ones would best suit the dress and proceeded to stand before the full-length mirror after putting on an oversized pair of red, high-heeled pumps.

"Yes, I guess this will have to do," the little princess said. Her excitement was beginning to waver as she spotted her unkempt hair and the dirty smudges on her cheeks.

"I just can't seem to get it right," she groaned. "I want to look absolutely beautiful for Daddy, but the day is passing so quickly. I haven't been able to make myself look the way I think I should. Daddy is the king, and everything must be perfect for him!"

The disappointed princess made a few passes with the back of her hand to remove the dirt from her face but gave up with a whimper.

"I guess I will see him anyway and tell him I am sorry. I hope he isn't too disappointed in me."

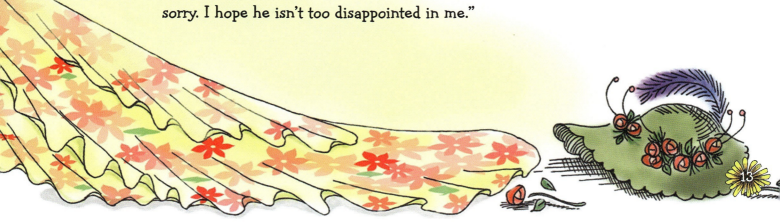

Moments later the little grown-up princess approached the grand and royal throne room. A tall, distinguished guard stood at attention in front of the double doors. As she approached, the guard's severe facial expression changed from one of duty and concentration to that of friendliness and welcome.

"Good morning, Your Highness," he said with a smile and a bit of a snicker. "You look quite lovely today, may I say!"

"Good morning," returned the princess, as she gave him a slightly embarrassed grin. "I want to say good morning to the king, please."

"Of course you may enter as you wish, but I must bring to your attention that many guests are already in the audience of His Majesty. He will most likely be very busy at this time."

"Oh, my! Am I already that late?" questioned the young princess. "I so wanted to see him before he got busy. I guess I took too much time doing other things."

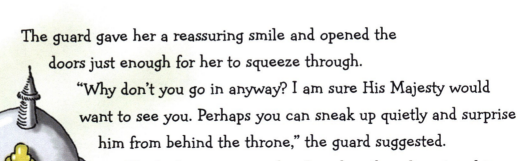

The guard gave her a reassuring smile and opened the doors just enough for her to squeeze through.

"Why don't you go in anyway? I am sure His Majesty would want to see you. Perhaps you can sneak up quietly and surprise him from behind the throne," the guard suggested.

The little princess took a deep breath and ventured in. She was astounded by the hundreds of finely dressed guests who had entered and were listening intently to the king. She stood still at the back of the largest room of the palace and took it all in, as if it were the first time she had been there.

"Dear, oh dear. Daddy will probably not even be able to speak with me. I must not interrupt him, as his business is so very important."

She sneaked all the way over to the left-hand wall and stood beneath a large portrait of her great-grandparents, all the while trying to decide what to do.

"Well, I think I shall give him just one little smile and a wave. If he doesn't have any time for me now, I will come back later. I understand how much he is needed!"

Each guest stood very still, both out of
respect for the king and also not wanting to
miss a single word of what he had to say. In
order to not disturb anyone or to draw any
attention to herself, the little princess slowly
and cautiously wove her way through the vast
crowd, all facing the front of the room. She
could hear the familiar voice of her father. To
every ear present, it was a strong, powerful, and
authoritative voice, but to the little princess it was
also the kindest and most loving voice she knew.

She looked up to find a clear path, but her view
was blocked by the dresses, hats, robes, and coats
of those who had gathered to honor her father.

"If I follow Daddy's voice, I will know
exactly where to go," she thought to herself
as she tiptoed between and around the most
fancily clad feet she had ever seen.

When she reached the front, the little
princess dashed behind a row of marble
pillars and rich drapes of royal blue.

"If I sneak up behind Daddy, I
can surprise him!" she planned.

"When he finishes speaking I can
tell him good morning!"

19

As the little princess slipped from behind one of the curtains near the back of the golden throne, she noticed the familiar right hand of her father extended out behind him. He continued to speak, as if she were not there, but he wiggled his fingers in a motion she knew all too well.

"Oh, he knew I was coming!" she thought. She put her tiny hand into his, and he drew her around to the front of the throne. He lifted her carefully and lovingly into his lap and held her close to his heart.

She leaned toward his head to whisper in his ear.

"It would be so fun to surprise you, Daddy, but you always seem to know when I am near," she said quietly.

"Yes, I know, my darling. But I can't help but wait for you to visit me each day," responded the king.

"Yes, Daddy. I am sorry it took me so long to get here today! I got distracted by my tea party. We were having such a nice chat. And then I had a very difficult time deciding what to wear. It seemed as if nothing was quite good enough for a visit with you. When I looked in the mirror, I realized I had forgotten to bathe last night. I know how you don't approve of someone coming before you dirty or unprepared. Please forgive me! I really love you, Daddy, and I just wanted to say good morning and give you a hug!"

As if there were no guests in the hall, or as if time did not matter, the king gathered her tightly in his powerful arms, and then he kissed her forehead.

"Sweet daughter of mine, you need never wait to come see me! It doesn't matter what you are wearing or if you think you will be accepted into my presence, because I want you to be with me all the time! You are mine, and that never changes!"

23

"When I look at you, my child, all I see is love!"

Made in the USA
Charleston, SC
03 June 2014